The GIRL With The Flaming Red Hair

ORLA KELLY
PUBLISHING

Written by Joyce Murphy

Illustrated by Aleksandra Bieniek

978-1-912328-77-2

JoyceMurphyAuthor.com

Orla Kelly Publishing
Kilbrody, Mount Oval
Rochestown, Cork
Ireland.

I am a Redhead and this book is my gift to all children with Red Hair. You are wonderful and you are unique, and I dedicate this book with love to you and your Hair.

This book belongs to

_____

_____

I am the Girl with the Flaming Red Hair
My name is Rosie Red
And I light up like a Flare

And when I am tucked up
And all cosy at night
It glows through my bedroom
Like a Firefly's Light

We are the Mammy and Daddy
Of the Girl with the Flaming Red Hair
We take her here – We take her there

We catch her hands
Run and say 1,2,3 .....
And up into the air
She flies with a Weeeeeeee

We are the friends
Of the Girl with the Flaming Red Hair
When first we met her
Boy did we stare?

Then she skippidy, hopidy hopped along
And we skipped behind her
Singing a Song

I am the Teacher
Of the Girl with the Flaming Red Hair

A real dreamer
Who looks out the window and stares

What do you dream about Dreamer Girl?
Skip skippidy, hopidy hop and a twirl

I am the Little Brother
Of the Girl with the Flaming Red Hair

We stay up real late
And we don't care

In bed our Mammy thinks we are asleep
While under the covers
We whisper and peek

I am the big Sister
Of the Girl with the Flaming Red Hair
Often Mammy and Daddy leave her in my care

Sometimes she is naughty

But when she is nice
I know she is coming to me for Advice

Advice on when her garden flowers will grow
Or why the ducks always swim in a row

Nature takes its time I Say
As I brush back her hair

One day you'll look out
And your flowers
Will just be there

I am the Grandma
Of the Girl with the Flaming Red Hair
When we are together
Oh what a pair

She lies on my tummy tum tum
And lays down to sleep
Then I pretend to be a dinosaur
And roar really deep

ROAR ....ROAR......ROAR

Grandma oh Grandma
She runs right away
And I chase her
Laughing all the way

When I catch her
I throw her up into the
air so high
That her hair flap, flap,
flaps
Like a bird in the sky

I am the Girl with the Flaming Red Hair
And I really love to accept a dare

So I dare you now children
Come visit me
And touch the Reddest Hair
You ever did see

To come and see
My nice little home

Just climb through the window
Drawn into this poem

Fun Facts about people with Flaming Red Hair

1. Less than 2% of the world's population has red hair.

2. 1 in 10 Irish people have red hair.

3. Scotland has the most Redheads living there with Ireland coming in second.

4. According to legend the first redhead in history, Prince Idon of Mu discovered the mythical land of Atlantis.

5. Redheads are more likely to be left handed.

6. Redheads produce their own Vitimin D which is good for your bones and teeth.

7. Redheads will never get grey hair.

About the Author

Joyce lives beside the sea in the South East of Ireland. As a child Joyce loved to make up imaginary lands where Queen Bears from lands full of honey grass and purple skies flew in red planes and visited her house on a Sunday. Sometimes they would leave apples, chocolate or small toys under the apple tree in her Nanny's back garden.

Starting at the age of ten Joyce wrote stories to escape into rich and colourful places that were filled with all kinds of adventures. Joyce has always been passionate about nourishing children's imagination and uniqueness. She also believes in supporting children to care for themselves, others and their environment. In her spare time she paddles in the sea, listens to whispers in seashells and dances in the rain.

To follow Joyce and find out more about her books, please visit www.joycemurphyautor.com.

Facebook - Joyce Murphy Author
Twitter - @JoyceMurphyM
Instagram - joycemurphyauthor

About the Illustrator

Aleksandra Bieniek is a self-taught digital artist from Limerick. By the time of publication she will have started the 4th year of animation degree in Limerick Institute of Technology. Besides illustrations she has a great passion for character design and 3D animation. This book is her first major illustration project and she's incredibly happy that she could be a part of it.

For more information, visit Aleksandra's Instagram and Twitter pages: @lewikdraws or http://bit.ly/lewikdraws

Please Review

Dear Reader,

If you enjoyed reading this book, would you kindly post a short review of the publication on Amazon or whatever book seller site you purchased from. Your feedback will make all the difference to getting the word out about this book.

To leave a review on Amazon, type in the book title and go to the book page. Please scroll to the bottom of the page to where it says 'Write a Review' and then submit your review.

Thank you in advance for your kindness.

Joyce

Made in the USA
Monee, IL
03 January 2023